Exploring Music

Percussion

Alyn Shipton

RSVP
RAINTREE
STECK-VAUGHN
PUBLISHERS
The Steck-Vaughn Company

Austin, Texas

Titles in the Series
Brass
Keyboards and Electronic Music
Percussion
Singing
Strings
Woodwinds

Edited by Pauline Tait
Picture research by Diana Morris
Designed by Julian Holland
Illustrator: Terry Hadler
Electronic Production: Scott Melcer

© **Copyright 1994, Steck-Vaughn Company**

All rights reserved. No part of the material protected by this copyright may be reproduced or utilized in any form or by any means, electronic or mechanical, including photocopying, recording, or by any information storage and retrieval system, without permission in writing from the copyright owner. Requests for permission to make copies of any part of the work should be mailed to: Copyright Permissions, Steck-Vaughn Company,
P.O. Box 26015, Austin, TX, 78755.

Picture acknowledgments

Raintree Steck-Vaughn Publishers would like to thank Edgarley Hall School music department, especially Mr. Brian Armfield, for assistance with commissioned photography; and David Titchener for supplying the photographs.

The author and publishers wish to thank the following photographic sources:
© Martha Cooper C.M. Dixon: p13 (bottom right), p22; Robert Harding Picture Library: p9 (top), p12, p14 (bottom), p29 (bottom); Michael Holford: p5; Viesti Associates: p28; Courtesy of Premier Percussion, Leicester/Neville Chadwick: title page, p10 (bottom left), p11; Redferns: p9 (bottom)/Odile Noel, p10 (top), p14 (top), p15, p20, p23 (bottom)/F. Coutrell, p25 (bottom), p29 (top)/M. Hutson; Courtesy of the South Bank Centre's Gamelan Education Programme at the Royal Festival Hall, London: p26/Chris Schwarz, p27/Rod Leon. The gamelan is a gift of the people of Indonesia to the people of Great Britain; Woodmansterne Picture Library: p17; Zefa: p4 (top); Courtesy of Zildjian: p19 (bottom)/Ian Croft.

Cover credits
(drums) Courtesy Premier Percussion, Leicester/Neville Chadwick;
(drummer) © Zefa.

Library of Congress Cataloging-in-Publication Data

Shipton, Alyn.
    Percussion / Alyn Shipton.
       p.   cm. — (Exploring music)
    Includes index.
    Summary: Describes various types of percussion instruments — including different drums, xylophones, cymbals, and shakers — discussing how they are played and their use in music around the world.
    ISBN 0-8114-2316-6
    1. Percussion instruments — Juvenile literature.   [1. Percussion instruments.]   I. Title.   II. Series: Shipton, Alyn. Exploring music.
ML1030.S55   1994
786.8'19—dc20
                                            93-20013
                                                  CIP
                                                 AC MN

Printed and bound in the United States
2 3 4 5 6 7 8 9 0 VHP 99 98 97 96 95

Contents

What Is a Percussion Instrument?	4
Homemade Percussion	6
The Xylophone	8
The Vibraphone	10
Drums	12
The Tom-Tom and the Bass Drum	14
The Timpani	16
Cymbals	18
The Drum Set	20
Unpitched Percussion	22
Percussion from Around the World	25
Glossary	30
Index	32

PERCUSSION

What Is a Percussion Instrument?

A percussion instrument is anything that makes a sound when you hit it. Whether it's struck with a stick, a mallet, your hand, or by thumping it on the ground, a percussion instrument sets up its sound waves when something hits it.

Percussion instruments fall into two group:

Tuned instruments play notes of a particular pitch. **Untuned** instruments are not intended to play any particular pitch.

TUNED PERCUSSION

Some percussion instruments are designed to play a note of the same pitch every time they are hit. Others can be adjusted, so that they can be tuned to play different notes.

The first group (the instruments that play particular notes when they are hit) includes the xylophone. It has bars of wood, each cut and shaped to play a note of the **scale** when struck with a mallet. In the second group are various drums. Drums have **"skins"** (or **heads**) that can be stretched to different **tensions** in order to make individual **notes**.

Tuned percussion can play melodies or play particular notes in a piece. Because percussion instruments are hit or struck to make their sound, each note stands out sharply from the rest.

This Korean drummer tunes her drum by adjusting the ropes at the side.

In this percussion group there are both tuned and untuned instruments. In front (left to right) are timpani, a xylophone, and the drums of the drum kit all of which are tuned. Behind, the triangle, cymbals, and woodblocks are untuned percussion.

4

WHAT IS A PERCUSSION INSTRUMENT?

Sound
When anything vibrates, it makes a sound. Our ears hear the sound because the air near the vibration is pushed or pulled and forms sound waves that carry it through the air.

There are three things about a sound that help us tell one from another:

volume: how loud it is;
pitch: how high or low it is; and
tone: the type or quality of the sound.

No two things vibrate in quite the same way, and the pattern of sound waves each object produces is unique. This means that when two different musical instruments play notes of the same volume and pitch, they will not sound the same.

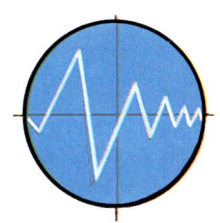

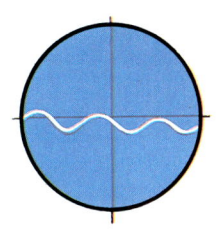

These oscilloscope pictures show the patterns of sound waves. On the left is the jagged pattern of noise made by an untuned instrument. On the right is the even pattern of a note played by a tuned musical instrument.

UNTUNED PERCUSSION

Performers and composers rely on percussion to supply **rhythm**. The percussion instruments that cannot play notes of a particular pitch are used to make rhythms, since they cannot play melodies or tunes. Some are played with sticks, or **beaters**, to make complex rhythms. Some are shaken to make repetitive patterns, and others make deep booming sounds that add depth and texture to music.

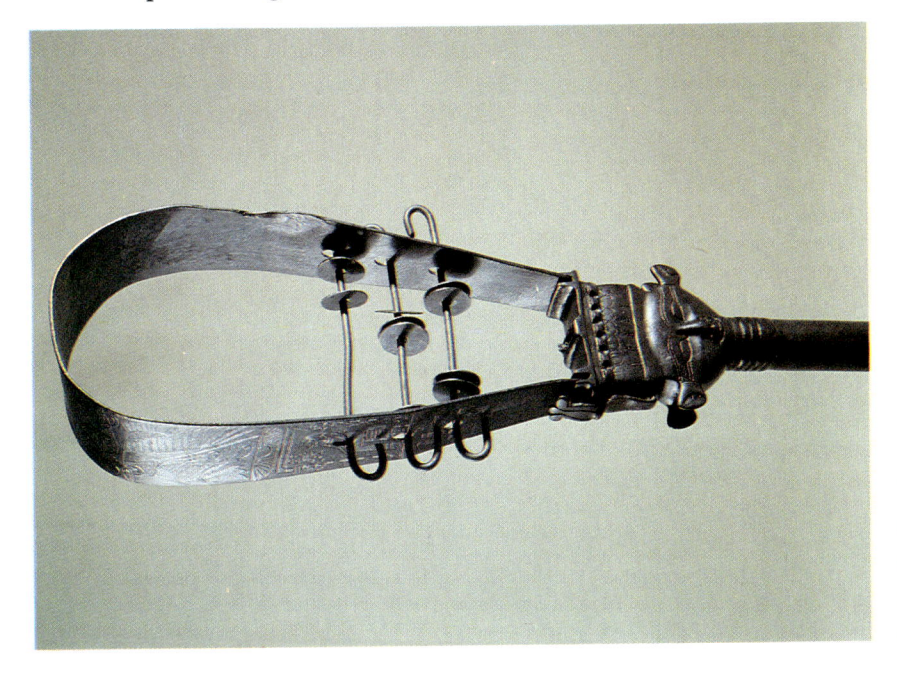

This early Egyptian *sistrum* from 850 B.C. was shaken to make the metal rings produce a tinkling sound. It is an untuned percussion instrument.

5

Homemade Percussion

Making Tuned Percussion

Anyone can make a tuned percussion instrument. The American drummer Spike Jones used to collect old bottles and cans for his "junkaphone," which was a kind of xylophone made of trash. You can do the same. Try putting together a group of bottles of different shapes and sizes, and arranging them in order according to the notes they play. With the high notes on your right and the low notes on your left, you should be able to learn how to play simple tunes.

One problem with bottles and jars of different shapes and sizes is that when you hit them with a beater they play notes that do not belong to the scale. If you want to make a "bottle-phone" that plays in tune, you need to collect a number of the same type of bottles—milk bottles or fruit-juice bottles. (Glass bottles are best.) Then pour a different amount of water into each bottle. This time, when you strike them, you'll find each bottle plays a different note. By adjusting the depth of the water, you can tune your instrument to play the notes of the scale.

The sound your instrument makes will change when the bottles are placed on different surfaces (say a mat or a shiny floor), and they will change even more if you suspend them from a frame using string.

TONE AND TIMBRE

The tone a percussion instrument has when it is hit changes when it stands on different surfaces, because each surface alters the way it vibrates. Hanging up a bottle so it is free on all sides changes the tone produced, because it is not vibrating against anything, and sound waves move out freely from it in all directions. Changing the depth of water inside a bottle changes the volume of air inside it that can move, and in this way changes the note produced. As you look at different percussion instruments, you will see that they are designed to vibrate in different ways. Some are held by hand, some have wooden frames, while others are suspended from stands.

Making Untuned Percussion

You can collect objects to make untuned percussion instruments, too. Large cans, turned upside down, will make good drums. Try stretching a piece of cloth or rubber sheeting over the open top of a large can. What happens to the note as the sheet gets tighter or looser? As well as drums, you can make simple shakers and rattles. Coffee cans can be filled with dried peas or gravel. When you shake them, they will make a good rhythmic sound. You can make a jingling rattle by threading bottle tops onto a coat hanger, or nailing them to a broom handle.

PERCUSSION

The Xylophone

The xylophone is a tuned percussion instrument, and its notes are made from bars of wood placed across a frame. An orchestral xylophone has its bars of wood positioned like piano keys. The diagram shows the layout. You can see from the smaller diagram how the notes are tuned. The shorter the bar, the higher the note. If the bar is made too short, the maker can deepen the sound again by carving away some of the underside of the bar.

The most interesting thing about the xylophone is what goes on underneath the frame. On page 7 we saw that the way a percussion instrument is allowed to vibrate changes its sound. Underneath the xylophone hangs a series of vertical tubes of different lengths. There is one for each note. The higher the pitch, the shorter the tube will be. The tubes are called **resonators**. They help to give the xylophone its distinctive or unique sound when the bars are struck with a wooden, metal, or rubber **mallet**. The small diagram gives a close-up of the resonator.

Smaller xylophones, like the kind often used in schools, do not have tube resonators. Instead they are built over a large wooden box that allows the notes to resonate.

The large concert xylophone has resonators, which you can see below the wooden "keys" of the instrument. The close-up shows how they fit.

8

THE XYLOPHONE

THE MARIMBA

The name marimba comes from central and southern Africa, where the word was used to describe a family of large xylophones. Today, we use the word to describe several kinds of xylophones used to play **folk** music in Africa and Latin America. The word is also used for a big version of the orchestral xylophone that was invented in the United States around 1910. Many folk marimbas use dried hollow gourds (or calabashes) as resonating tubes, which make them look unusual and often very colorful.

Listening Guide

Xylophone parts have been written by Puccini (in his opera *Turandot*), and Saint-Saëns in *Danse macabre* (to represent a skeleton!). Marimbas have been used by Percy Grainger ("In a Nutshell") and Milhaud, who wrote a concerto for it. The famous jazz musician Lionel Hampton plays the marimba and the vibraphone.

A traditional South American marimba. Larger versions of these instruments can have two or three players.

Xylophone Playing

Most orchestral percussionists play the xylophone as well as untuned percussion. To begin, you can pick out simple tunes with the mallets, but professional players use two mallets in each hand and play very rapidly. You'd find it helpful to study the piano or keyboard to be an effective xylophone player like the brilliant soloist Evelyn Glennie (left).

PERCUSSION

The Vibraphone

The vibraphone (or "vibes," as it is called by musicians) has a ringing sound, and the instrument is very popular in jazz. It is like an ordinary orchestral xylophone with its wooden bars swapped for metal ones. There is a set of revolving disks inside the top of the resonating tubes to make the sound they produce throb and pulsate. The diagram shows how the disks revolve inside the resonating tubes, and how the bars themselves are suspended on elastic rope above the frame.

Because the vibraphone's bars are made of metal, it is called a "metallophone." There are other tuned percussion instruments in the orchestra that also have metal keys or notes.

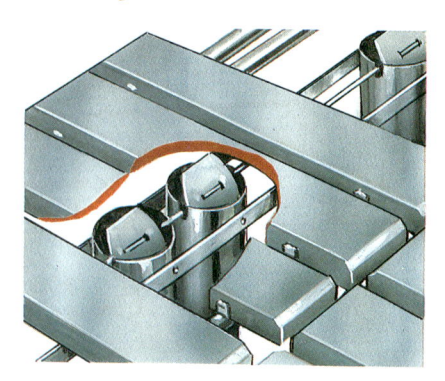

Jazz vibraphone player Gary Burton

THE GLOCKENSPIEL

The notes of a glockenspiel are arranged like those of a xylophone. They are made of steel and rest on strips of felt. The instrument has a flat wooden case and no resonating tubes. Its clear ringing sound has been used by many composers to represent the sound of bells. Another version of the glockenspiel is designed to be carried on a frame, and is known as the "bell-lyra."

Two modern glockenspiels, showing their flat cases and metal bars

10

TUBULAR BELLS

At the back of the orchestral percussion section, you can often see a tall frame containing metal tubes that look like straight pieces of scaffolding. These are tubular (or orchestral) bells, and they are tuned to produce the notes of the scale when each one is hit on its metal cap with a **hammer**. The hammer is covered in leather or is sometimes made of heavy plastic. The tubular bells are often used by composers to imitate the sound of church bells. They appear in orchestral music, like the *Symphonie fantastique* by Berlioz, or operas, like Britten's *The Turn of the Screw*.

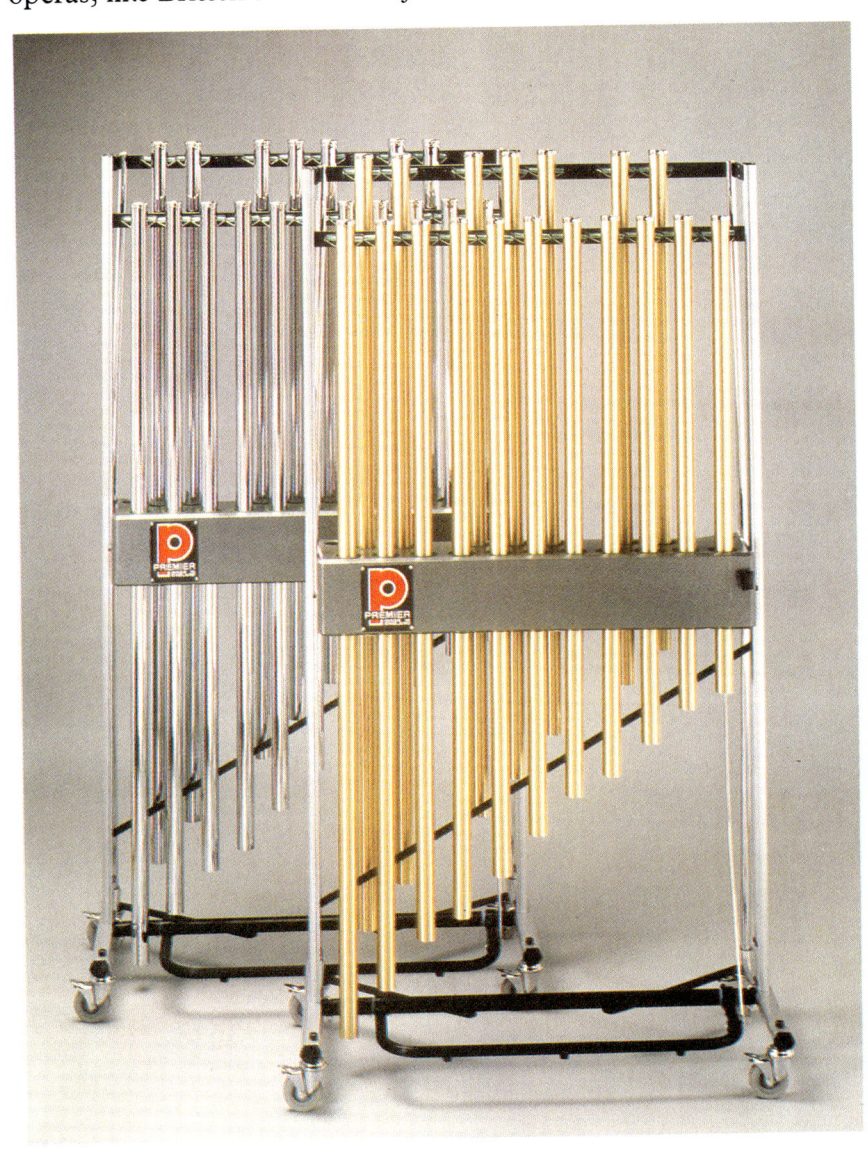

If you look at the tops of these two sets of tubular bells, you can see that they are staggered like the black and white keys of a piano to help the player hit the right notes.

CROTALES

These are tiny cymbals that are struck together, or with a beater, to produce clear ringing notes. They were popular in ancient Greece and Rome (see p. 22), and were made in **sets** of different sizes. Today, they are made in sets that play the notes of the scale. Ravel, Berlioz, and Debussy used them in their music.

Listening Guide

You can hear the vibraphone played on jazz records by Lionel Hampton, Red Norvo, and Milt Jackson of the Modern Jazz Quartet. French composers like Darius Milhaud and Maurice Ravel have written for the vibraphone. The glockenspiel often can be heard in military bands.

PERCUSSION

Drums

Drums are among the oldest instruments in the world. All drums have a frame across which is stretched a tight skin, or head. The player beats the head to make a sound.

Two main things change the sound a drum makes: One is the size and shape of the shell; the other is the tension of the head. Most drum heads are mounted on hoops. These hoops are placed over the open shell of the drum and then held in place with an outer wooden or metal hoop. The outer hoop has ropes or metal clamps attached to it that can be tightened. This is how the tension of the head is changed and the notes it plays are altered.

THE SNARE DRUM

If you see a military band march along, you'll see two types of drums. There are the huge **bass** drums (see page 14) and usually a group of snare, or parade, drums. The snare drum was developed in the 16th century and is still carried in the same way, on a sling that holds it on the player's left side, just below the waist. Both hands are left free to hold a pair of **sticks,** and snare drummers play using both sticks together. Drummers practice rhythm patterns using their sticks in different sequences. The most common pattern is the **roll**.

DRUMS

The top head of the snare drum is called the "batter head," as it is the one struck by the sticks. Underneath the drum is another head, and attached to it is a mechanism with a set of wire springs that run across the width of the drum. This mechanism is called the **snare,** and it is designed to rattle against the lower head every time the drum is struck with the sticks. The snare adds a crisp attacking sound to the drum. This kind of drum is sometimes called the side drum.

In the orchestra, and as part of the modern rock drum kit, the snare drum is held on a stand at waist height in front of the player. In some orchestral music, and a lot of jazz, the snare drum is played with two wire brushes instead of sticks.

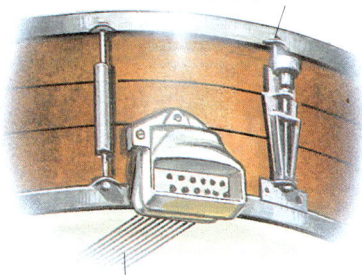

This is the modern snare drum on its stand.

THE TENOR DRUM
In old prints and pictures of marching bands, some side drummers are shown playing a drum that is bigger than the modern snare drum. The large side drum, which does not have a snare, is called the **tenor** drum.

THE TABOR
The ancestor of the modern snare is the tabor. It looks like a tenor drum, but most tabors have a snare on the top head. In the Middle Ages, pipe and tabor players were often heard together.

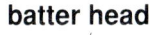

A soldier from the English Civil War, in the mid 1600s, plays a tabor.

PERCUSSION

The Tom-Tom and the Bass Drum

Tom-toms, or timbales as they are sometimes called, are single-headed drums with no snares. They are made in sets for orchestral playing and usually in twos or threes for rock and jazz drum sets. Small tom-toms are sometimes mounted on top of bass drums in a drum set. More often, they stand on three adjustable legs. These tom-toms with legs are called "floor-toms" by drummers. Composers use the tom-tom to represent the traditional drums of Africa, or of Native Americans. In jazz, Gene Krupa used tom-toms in Benny Goodman's "Sing Sing Sing," and Duke Ellington's drummer Sonny Greer played them in "Caravan."

This is a set of four orchestral tom-toms in the middle of a busy percussion section.

THE BASS DRUM

The large and ungainly bass drum is the deepest-sounding member of the percussion section of the orchestra. The modern bass drum is up to 40 inches (100 cm) in diameter and has a calfskin or plastic head on each side. In early drums, the tension of the heads was adjusted using ropes. This is still done in marching bands, where it is important to keep the weight of the drum as light as possible. For orchestras and other uses, the bass drum has metal **tensioning rods**.

The note a bass drum plays is altered by the tension of the head. The tone of the drum is altered by the kind of beater the player uses. A soft beater produces a dull, deep note; a harder beater makes a louder sound, like the noise of the cannons in Tchaikovsky's *1812 Overture*.

The military bass drummer often gives the signal to the band to start and finish playing.

14

THE TOM-TOM AND THE BASS DRUM

In jazz and rock drum sets, the bass drum is mounted on the floor, and the player uses a foot pedal to operate the beater. In the orchestra, the bass drum is usually supported on a large stand, which allows it to be moved easily and to be swiveled into the best position for playing.

Listening Guide

One of the most famous pieces that uses the snare drum is Ravel's *Bolero*, where the snare plays the same short phrase 169 times! The whole drum section of the orchestra is used for the gun battle in Aaron Copland's ballet *Billy the Kid*. Drums are used in many funeral marches—Berlioz asks for six muffled drums in his march from *Hamlet*. Dramatic moments can be made more dramatic with drums. In Verdi's *Requiem*, the "Dies Irae" has powerful moments for the bass drum.

In jazz, listen to the marching bands of New Orleans like the Dirty Dozen Brass Band. They use separate bass and snare drum players as their percussion section. Jazz drummers like Buddy Rich and Jo Jones were great snare drummers.

Buddy Rich

PERCUSSION

The Timpani

The timpani, or "timps," are drums that can be tuned to a precise pitch, and which are usually called kettle drums because of their characteristic shape. The heads of the timpani are stretched over frames made of copper or fiberglass that are more or less hemispherical, like a ball cut in half. In the late 18th century these copper drums were supported on three metal legs. Modern fiberglass timps are supported in cradles of fiberglass, with casters or wheels to make them easy to move.

There are two main types of timpani. One kind uses screw tensioning to tighten the drum heads and tune them to particular notes. The other kind, invented to allow the timpanist to change notes quickly, has a pedal that adjusts the skin tension of the drum. It also operates a small gauge to show the musician the note that will sound when the drum is hit. Fine adjustment to pedal timps is made with a special tuning key that tightens or loosens the head of the drum. You can sometimes see the timpanist in an orchestra lean over and "whisper" to the drums. In fact, he or she is quietly singing or humming a note. When the drum is tuned to the same note it booms back, helping the percussionist tune it precisely for performances. The pedal also allows the timpanist to change the note as the drum is being played, making a slur or **glissando** (a frequent effect on comic film soundtracks).

The two kinds of timpani: The upper picture shows a pedal timpani; the lower drum has screw tensioning.

Timpani Playing

All orchestral percussionists want to play the timps, since they are among the most frequently used percussion instruments. The usual orchestra has three timpani, although sometimes composers expect there to be four or five. Then the percussionist is kept busy retuning the drums to play different notes and following the music at the same time. By using different kinds of beaters, the sound of the timpani can be changed greatly, although normally mallets with large felt heads are used. If you want to balance on a horse and play timpani at the same time, then the mounted bands might have the job for you!

Listening Guide

Haydn began his *Symphony No. 103* with the timpani, and it has been called the "drumroll symphony" for years. Many of Haydn and Mozart's orchestral works include the timpani. Timpani are also used in symphonies by all the major classical composers. Walton's *Symphony No. 1* has a duet for two timpanists, and some composers, like Robert Parris and Elliott Carter, have written solos for the timpani.

PERCUSSION

Cymbals

Cymbals cannot be tuned to a particular pitch. They are metal discs of various sizes, usually made of a mixture of copper and tin. In the orchestra, and in many military and marching bands, cymbals are played in pairs. Each cymbal is slightly convex (curved outward), so that only their outer edges touch when they are clashed together in a vertical sweeping movement. The cymbals are made with a shallow "cut" in the middle. The player's hand slips into a leather strap that threads through a central hole in the cymbal. After crashing the cymbals together, the orchestral percussionist will sometimes hold them up in the air to "ring" until they stop vibrating. Orchestras also use "suspended" cymbals. These hang from their straps on a special stand or are supported through their central hole. The player uses drumsticks or soft mallets to get a range of effects. Using two mallets to play a roll can produce a tremendous roar.

The orchestral cymbals. You can just see the leather straps that the player uses to hold them.

CYMBALS

CYMBALS IN THE DRUM SET
Jazz and rock drummers never clash pairs of cymbals together like an orchestral percussionist. Instead, they have a wide array of cymbals on stands around their drums, each of which does a different job.

THE RIDE CYMBAL
Jazz drummers keep a background rhythm going throughout a piece by hitting the **ride cymbal** with a drumstick. The cymbal got its name from being used to "ride" through an entire piece. Ride cymbals have a clear ringing tone, and they are between 18 and 24 inches (45 and 60 cm) in diameter. Some drummers put rivets through them, or put chains over them to sustain the sound longer, making an effect called the "sizzle."

THE SPLASH CYMBAL
The jazz drummer who wants to get the same effect as crashing two cymbals together uses a small-diameter ringing cymbal called a "crash" or "splash" cymbal. When hit with a drumstick, it makes a dramatic short, sharp sound.

The Triangle
Many percussionists use the triangle, a triangular shaped piece of metal, to produce a clear ringing sound. It has to be hit with a metal stick.

This drummer has all three kinds of cymbals in his kit. The ride cymbals are the wider ones suspended above him. He has two hi-hats, one to his left and one to his right, and three splash cymbals, two above him and one on the extreme left.

THE HI-HAT
The hi-hat is a pair of cymbals set together on a stand so they can be clashed together by using a foot pedal. The drummer can use the hi-hat to play cymbals while keeping both hands free to play other parts of the drum set. Jo Jones, the jazz drummer of Count Basie's band, made the hi-hat the basis of modern big-band jazz drumming by using it to play the four-beats of every bar. Originally, hi-hats were called "sock" cymbals, or "Charleston" cymbals, and they were first used in the 1920s.

PERCUSSION

The Drum Set

Beginning around the end of World War I, jazz and dance band drummers wanted to put a group of percussion instruments together into a set. Instead of a whole orchestral percussion section, just one person could play the bass drum, snare drum, tom-toms, and cymbals.

Pioneer drummers like Baby Dodds and Tony Sbarbaro used drum kits that had giant bass drums. Mounted on them were crash and ride cymbals and a Chinese tom-tom. A range of woodblocks and bells were also fixed to the top of this drum, and a stand on the drummer's left held a military snare drum.

By the 1930s, drummers were playing sets of drums that look very much like the drums used by rock drummers today. Sonny Greer (with Duke Ellington) and Chick Webb (who led his own band) had enormous drum sets, with everything from timpani to chime bars. In the diagram opposite, you can see one of these huge sets of drums. It includes a number of tuned percussion instruments, as well as a number of other members of the percussion family. The tam-tams and tubular bells were rarely used but looked wonderful.

Jazz drummer Elvin Jones is shown here with a standard modern drum set. He has a bass drum, snare drum (partly hidden), and four tom-toms (two are mounted on the bass drum; two are "floor toms" and stand alone).

THE DRUM SET

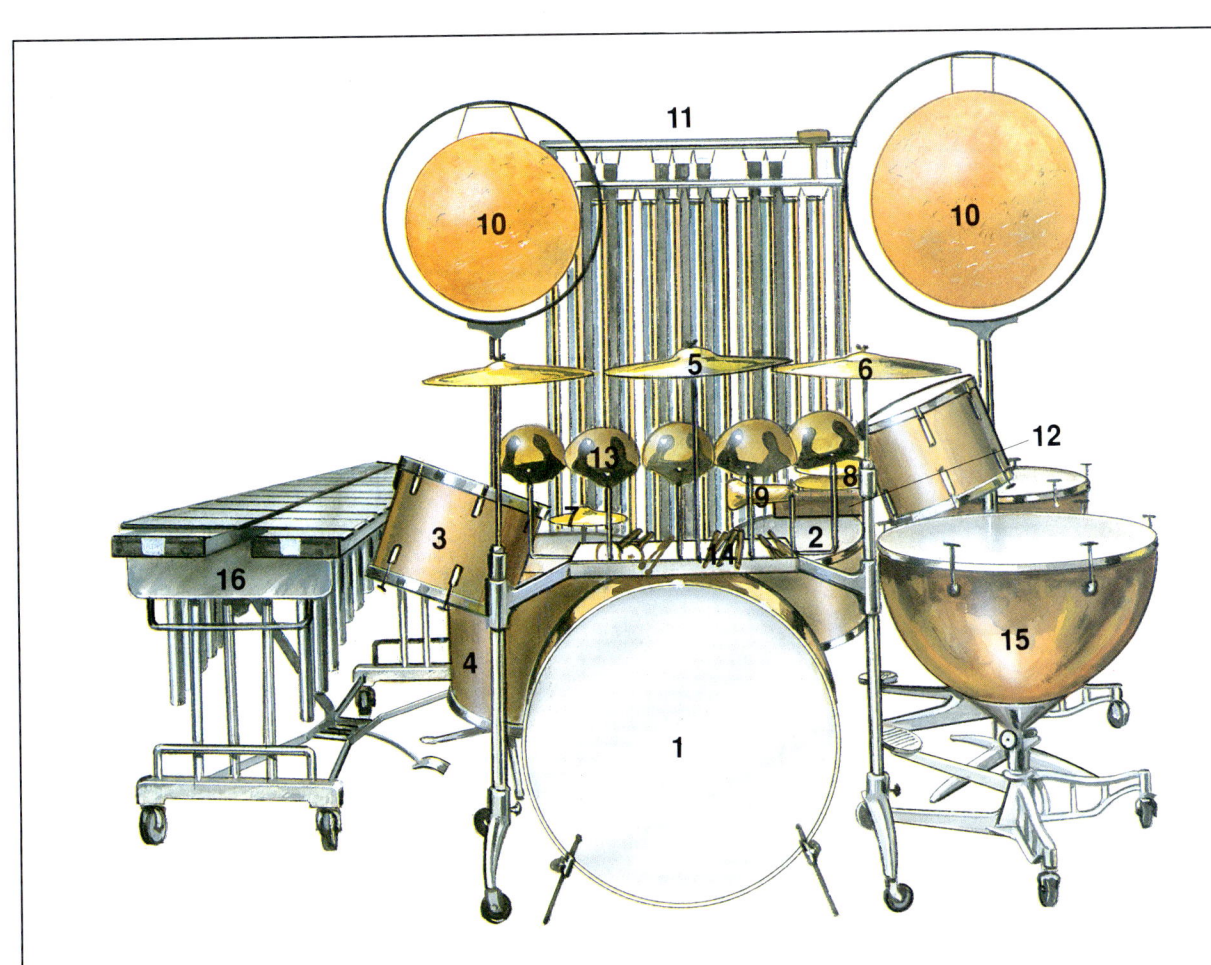

1. Bass Drum. In drum sets, these instruments were often painted with anything from a sunset to a portrait of the drummer or bandleader.
2. Snare Drum
3. Drum-mounted tom-tom
4. Floor tom-tom
5. Large crash or Chinese cymbals
6. Ride or Turkish cymbals
7. Small crash or splash cymbal
8. Hi-hat cymbal
9. Cow-bell. Just like the bells worn by cows in the Alps, these are mounted on a stand clamped to the bass drum.
10. Tam-tams. These are huge Chinese gongs. Gongs like these appear in the orchestra and also in East Asian music.
11. Tubular bells
12. Woodblock (slit drum) (see page 23)
13. Temple blocks or "skulls" (see page 23)
14. Tray for sticks and mallets on what is called the drummer's "console." (Today these are often kept in a felt bag suspended from one of the tom-toms.)
15. Pair of pedal timpani
16. Vibraphone

PERCUSSION

Unpitched Percussion

In the orchestra and in the drum set there are several familiar percussion instruments that are used in many parts of the world in children's percussion bands, or in special **compositions** for children's orchestras.

THE TAMBOURINE

The tambourine is a simple "frame drum." It has a shallow frame like a hoop, with a skin or head on one side only. The head is pinned or nailed to the drum, which means it cannot be tuned. Usually there are metal disks, or "jingles," set into openings in the frame. The tambourine is shaken to give a jingling effect, and the head can be struck in several different ways with the player's hand or with sticks. This makes it a very versatile member of the percussion family, and it has been popular since it was used in ancient Egyptian music to mourn the dead. More recently, it appeared in Spanish and gypsy folk music. Composers since Mozart have used it for folk music effects in the orchestras. In William Walton's *Façade* only the jingles are played. In Tchaikovsky's *Nutcracker* ballet music, the tambourine is played in many different ways: shaken, struck, and "rolled" with the thumb.

This mosaic from Pompeii, Italy, shows a Roman musician (right) playing a tambourine about 1,800 years ago. In the center is a *crotales* player, and behind these two figures is a woman playing a pair of woodwind pipes.

UNPITCHED PERCUSSION

THE WOODBLOCK
The simplest woodblock used in the orchestra is a rectangular block of wood with a long slit cut into the side. Other kinds of woodblocks include sets of temple blocks or "skulls," like the ones shown on the drum kit on page 21. Woodblocks are made in sets of various sizes. Although they do not play notes of precise pitch, the largest make a deep "clop" sound, while the smaller varieties make a higher "clip." As well as being used for comic effects in jazz and dance bands, composers have often used the woodblock to create the sound of horses' hooves or clog dances.

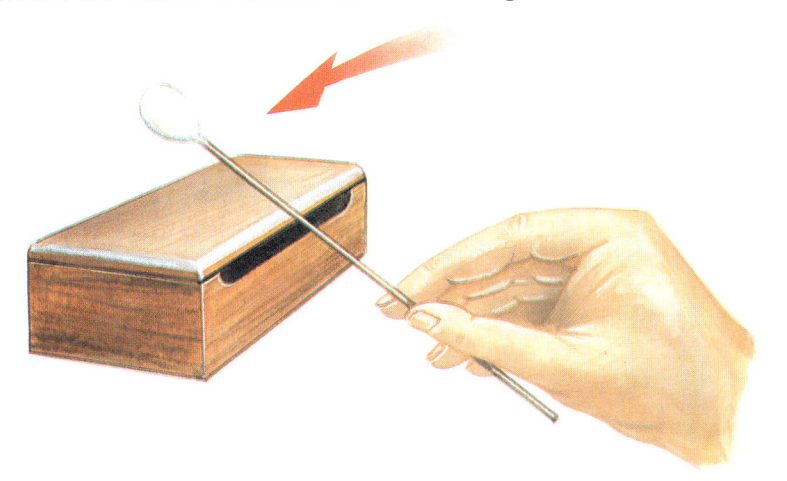

Woodblock

THE CASTANETS
The orchestral castanets have two shallow cups of wood mounted on a wooden handle to make a simple clapper. The player holds the handle in one hand and shakes the instrument against the other. This is an easy instrument to play, but the type of castanets used by Spanish folk dancers requires far more skill. They have no handle; instead, the player holds and plays both shallow cups in one hand. The cups are joined by a cord that loops around the thumb, and the best players make fast and complex rhythms. Composers like Bizet (in *Carmen*) and Chabrier (in *España*) use the castanets to conjure up the image of Spain.

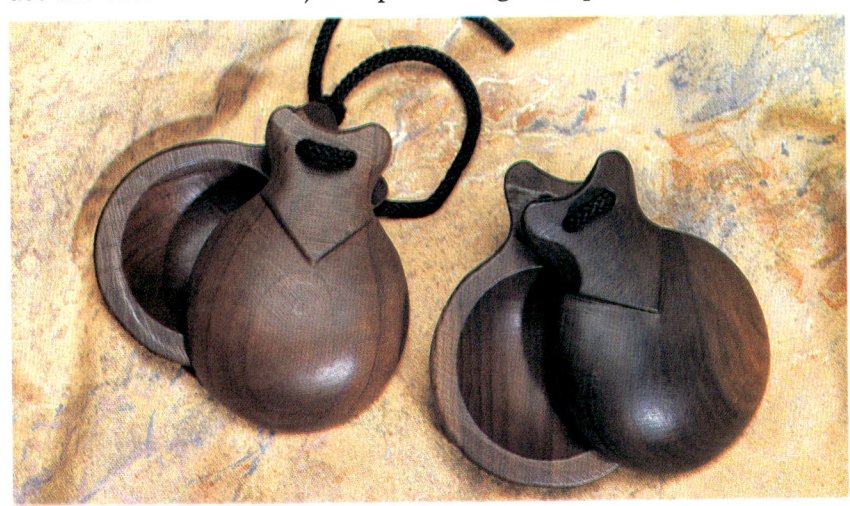

Two pairs of Spanish folk castanets. A player would hold one pair in each hand.

PERCUSSION

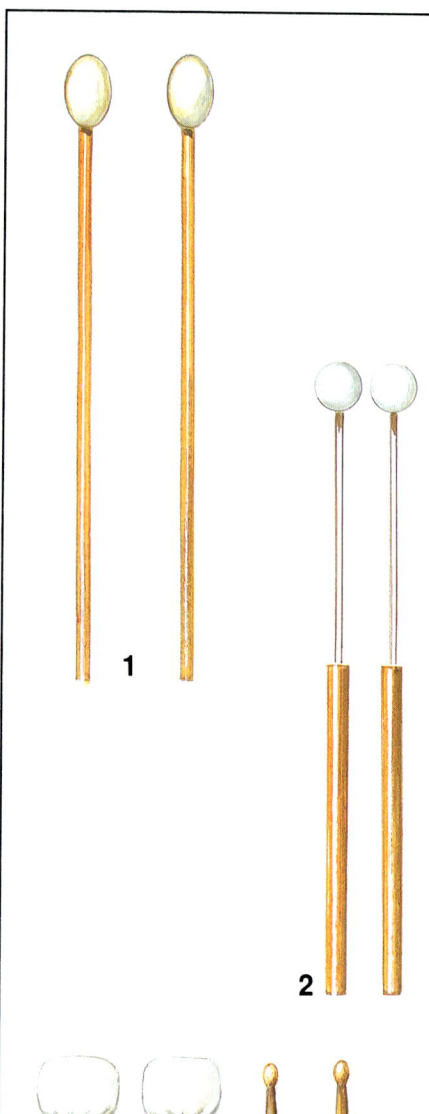

Sticks and Beaters

Because percussion instruments make their sound when they are hit or struck, a lot of thought has gone into the sticks and mallets that are used to hit or beat percussion.

1. and **2.** Vibraphone and glockenspiel mallets. These are similar in design, but the ends are different. The vibes mallets have softer tips than the hard wooden or metal ends of the glockenspiel beaters.
2. Timpani mallets. These have felt-covered ends fixed to sticks wider than snare drumsticks. This way the player can grip them and balance the mallets properly to control timpani rolls.
3. Snare drumsticks. These are what we all think of as "drumsticks," and they're used for snare drums, tenor drums, tabors, and tom-toms. They come in a range of sizes and thicknesses, and each is cut from a single piece of wood, its tip shaped to a suitable thickness and weight. Some snare drumsticks have tips hardened with nylon or wax.
4. Snare drum brushes. These look like a cross between a whisk and a small broom. They have strands of wire or nylon that retract, or go back, into the handle for storage and travel.
5. Bass drum mallets. These are like timpani mallets, but they're usually shorter and stockier. Their heads are made in varying degrees of hardness.
6. Tubular bells mallet. This is a large leather or plastic hammer.

Percussion from Around the World

Latin American Percussion
There are many unusual percussion instruments found in different corners of the globe. Some of the most unusual percussion effects are made by instruments from Central and South America. The main types are shakers and scrapers.

Shakers
The two most widely used Latin American shakers are the *maracas* and the *cabaca*. They are similar in shape, but the *maracas* have their beads or buckshot inside a gourd or wooden shell fixed to a handle. The *cabaca* has beads strung in rows on the outside. It is similar to the gourd covered with a mesh of shells or seeds that came from Africa. When either instrument is shaken, the beads or buckshot rattle against the gourd. Skilled players can set up an insistent, repetitive rhythm that is used as a backing for groups and singers.

Maracas

Zydeco bands from Louisiana once used ordinary washboards as rhythm instruments. Now, players like this one wear specially made "washboard vests" that are played with bottle openers (like this) or by putting thimbles on their fingertips.

Scrapers
Scrapers are also used to set up a regular backing rhythm. Mostly, they consist of ridged surfaces that are scraped or rubbed with a stick. The two most common types are the *guiro* and the *reco-reco*. The same effect can be made with a household washboard.

PERCUSSION

GAMELAN

In the Indonesian islands of Java and Bali there is a tradition of large orchestras made up almost entirely of percussion instruments. The gamelan, as such a group is called, has gongs, chimes, xylophones, drums, and cymbals. Sometimes there are singers and woodwinds as well, but when you look at a gamelan, the main thing you will notice is the huge array of percussion. Nobody is certain when or how gamelan music began, but archaeologists have found remains of **ensembles** from over 1,000 years ago.

Gamelan orchestras are set carefully, with a regular pattern. The plan shows how the various instruments are arranged. The instruments are tuned to different scales. Some have five notes, and some have seven.

Children in their own gamelan ensemble.

A. small metal xylophones (like glockenspiels)
B. suspended gongs
C. horizontal gongs
D. gong chimes
E. large metal xylophone
F. xylophone
G. drums
H. singer, choir, other instruments

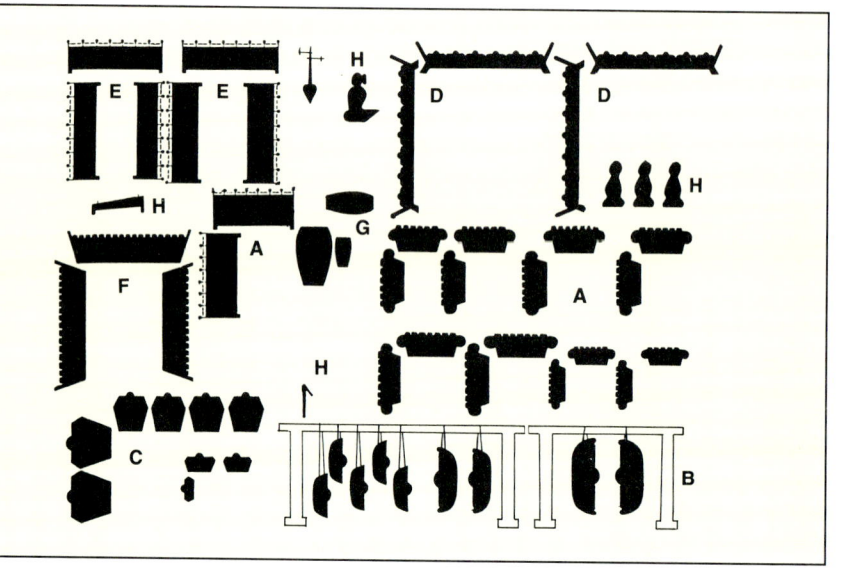

How the Gamelan is Used

For hundreds of years, gamelan orchestras have been used for religious ceremonies, for dances, and for shadow theater. When they are in the open air, they include more raucous, strident instruments: drums and gongs with loud oboes and shawms as well. For indoor performances, they have different instruments—quiet xylophones, chimes, and flutes.

In central Java gamelan ensembles were used in ceremonies to try to bring rain to water the rice fields. In other parts of the islands, they are more often used for wedding celebrations, although today you might find everybody happily listening to a tape recording instead of the real thing! Gamelan music is so important in some parts of Bali and Java that the instruments are regarded as sacred.

In many parts of Bali, gamelan orchestras were often in temples, while in Java they were set up in courts. Over the years, they have spread from temples and courts into villages, many of which have their own ensemble.

It is possible to get an enormous range of sound from all the instruments of the gamelan. One of the most dramatic gamelan pieces is the *prajuritan*, the 15th-century story of a huge battle between two kingdoms.

An original Indonesian gamelan orchestra.

PERCUSSION

WEST INDIAN STEEL BAND

The unique sound of a Caribbean carnival always includes music from a steel band. These bands have special tuned drums carefully beaten out of metal oil barrels. Great care must be taken when making each drum so as not to ignite old fuel vapor. Sparks can be very dangerous. The drum is cut in half, and shallow depressions are beaten into the flat surface of the top or bottom, in the shape of small circles. Each circle plays a different note. They are hammered into different sizes, and when each circle is hit with a beater, it produces a clear ringing sound. The size of the oil drum determines the range of notes it can produce. Small drums play higher notes; larger drums sound deeper.

Often, a steel band plays to create the right carnival atmosphere.

PERCUSSION FROM AROUND THE WORLD

HARRY PARTCH
One of the most unusual figures in music was the Californian inventor Harry Partch. He designed and made his own instruments, many of which were strange and wonderful percussion. He used scales of notes that are different from the normal octave and built instruments to play all these unusual pitches. His giant marimbas and his gourd tree make unusual sounds on records of his own music.

CONGA DRUM
In Afro-Cuban music, the drums are often tall, barrel-shaped wooden instruments played with the fingers. They usually come in pairs, and they have found their way into most Latin American dance orchestras and Latin jazz bands.

TABLA
In classical Indian music, the most important percussion instrument is the *tabla*. This is a pair of small hand-played drums, somewhat like the timpani in shape. The **treble** right-hand drum has a tapered wooden frame, while the large left-hand bass drum has a metal or pottery frame.

African frame drums, which are a kind of conga drum, are worn on a sling over the player's shoulder.

The black disks seen on the skins of the *tabla* are tuning paste to give harmonic overtones. The *sitar,* a member of the lute family, often accompanies the *tabla*.

KULINTANG
The *kulintang* is somewhat like some of the gongs in the gamelan. It is the gong-chime of the Philippines. Orchestras of gong-chimes are called *kulintang* as well. The most common form looks like a row of saucepans. The gongs are hung on two strings stretched across a wooden frame. On the top of each gong is a raised lump, or "boss." The size of this boss, which varies from about 1 to 1.25 inches (2.5 to 3 cm) is what changes the note. The gongs are played with soft wooden mallets.

PERCUSSION

Glossary

bass — lowest range of notes sung by an adult male voice

beater — an implement used for striking a percussion instrument, also known as a drumstick

composition — making up and writing a piece of music

ensemble — a group of instrumental players

folk — music based on traditional tunes and songs

glissando — a slide or "glide" through all the notes of an instrument. On tuned percussion it is made by sliding a beater along the bars, and on timpani by releasing or increasing the tension immediately after striking the head

hammer — hammer-shaped beater used on tubular bells

head — see **skin**

mallet — beater used on glockenspiel, vibraphone, xylophone, or *marimba*

note — a musical sound

pitch — value of a note indicated by its position on the scale

resonator — the part of an instrument that amplifies its sound and makes it louder or stronger

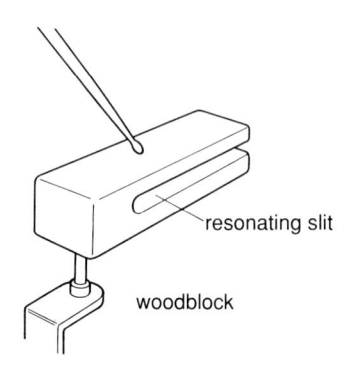

resonating slit
woodblock

rhythm — the division of time in music. A rhythmic pattern is a succession of notes of different length.

ride cymbals — cymbals used in jazz to carry the beat

roll — repeated strokes on a drum made with two beaters or sticks

scale — steplike, ordered arrangement of pitches used in music

set — number of instruments that belong together, or a number of examples of the same instrument in different sizes

skin — tightly stretched membrane

GLOSSARY

snare   wires that lie against the lower head of a side drum and vibrate when the batter-head is struck

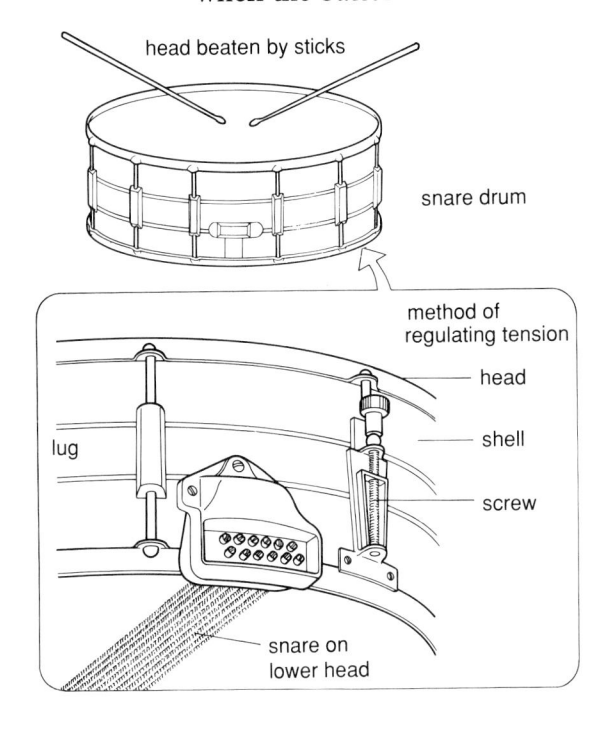

stick   a beater for a drum

tenor   highest range of notes sung by an adult male voice

tension   even stretching of the head to produce the right pitch or tone

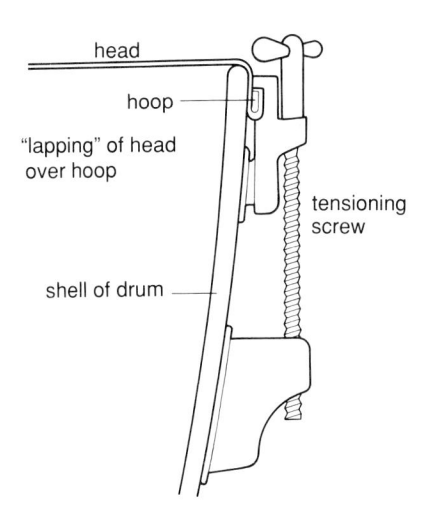

tensioning rod   threaded rod that adjusts the tension of the drum head

timbre   characteristic quality of sound produced by a particular instrument

tone   quality of sound

treble   an instrument having the highest range in one family of instruments

tuned percussion   an instrument that plays notes of a particular pitch

untuned percussion   an instrument that is not meant to play at any particular pitch

volume   the loudness or softness of a sound

PERCUSSION

Index

beaters 5, 6, 11, 14, 15, 17, 24, 28
bell 10, 20
  cow 21
  tubular 11, 20, 21, 24
bell-lyra 10
bottle-phone 6
brushes 13, 24
castanets 23
chimes 20, 26, 27, 29
crotales 11, 22
cymbal 4, 11, 18-21, 26
  crash 19-21
  hi-hat 19, 21
  ride 19-21
  splash 19, 21
dance band 20, 23
drum 4, 7, 12-17, 20, 26-29
  bass 12, 14, 15, 20, 21, 24
  conga 29
  kettle 16
  snare 12-15, 20, 21, 24
  tenor 13, 24
drum roll 12, 17
drum skin 4, 12, 22
folk music 9, 22
foot pedal 15, 19
gamelan 26, 27, 29
glockenspiel 10, 11, 24, 26
gong 21, 26, 27, 29
gourd 9, 25, 29
hammer 11, 24
jazz 10, 11, 13-15, 19, 20, 23, 29
kulintang 29
mallet 4, 8, 9, 17, 18, 21, 24, 29

maracas 25
marching band 14, 15, 18
marimba 9, 11, 29
metallophone 10
military band 11, 12, 14, 17, 18
orchestra 8-11, 13-20, 22, 26
rattles 7
resonators 8, 10
rock music 13-15, 20
scrapers 25
shakers 7, 25
sistrum 5
sitar 29
sound waves 5
steel band 28
sticks 4, 5, 12, 13, 18, 19, 21, 24
tabla 29
tabor 13, 24
tambourine 22
tam-tams 20, 21
temple blocks 21,
tension 4, 12, 14
timpani 4, 16, 20, 24
  pedal 16, 21
tom-tom 14, 20, 21, 24
  drum mounted 14, 20, 21
  floor 14, 20, 21
triangle 4, 19
vibraphone 10, 11, 21, 24
washboard 25
woodblock 4, 20, 21, 23
xylophone 4, 8, 9, 26, 27

© 1993 Zoë Books Limited

786.8 SHI	Shipton, Alyn. Percussion		12135
			$15.98

DATE DUE	BORROWER'S NAME	ROOM NO.

786.8 SHI   Shipton, Alyn.   12135

Percussion

LONGFELLOW ELEM SCHOOL
HOUSTON TX 77025

644607 01598   10236C